You could be a **dragon**
Guarding all their jewels.

I could be the **king** or **queen**
Making all the rules,

I Could Be, You Could Be

Written by **Karen Owen**   Illustrated by **Barroux**

Barefoot Books
step inside a story

I could be a **parakeet**
Perching in a tree,

You could swing
on a curly tail —

Like a cheeky monkey.

I could be an alien
With a funny face,

You could be an **astronaut**
Zooming into space.

As a topsy-turvy clown,

You could be an Arab pony

Prancing
up
and
down.

I could be a **dolphin**
Swimming in the sea,

But the best thing
I could ever be...

...is ME!

Mask Making and Make Believe

Pretending to be someone else is fun – and making a mask out of recycled materials can make it even more exciting. Ask an adult to help transform you into a chimpanzee, a horse, a clown or even an alien by following these simple instructions:

What to find:
* cereal or other card boxes
* a ruler or tape measure
* a pencil
* a large plate (optional)
* scissors
* non-toxic glue
* non-toxic paints, felt tip pens or crayons
* scraps and bric-a-brac (create a rummage box with leftover bits of wool, foil, tissue paper, fabric, buttons, stamps – anything goes!)
* elastic

Or make yourself a crown!

What to do:
1. Use a tape measure or ruler to measure the width and height of your face and the position of your eyes.

2. Take a piece of the cereal box and use the measurements you have made to draw a simple, round template, including the eyes. You can draw around the edge of a big plate to create a well-rounded mask.

3. Use the scissors to cut out the mask, eye holes and holes for the elastic.

4. Use paints, felt tip pens or crayons to decorate your mask.

5. When the paint has dried, add bits of bric-a-brac and leave the mask to dry.

6. Tie a knot in one end of the elastic and thread it through one hole, from the front of the mask to the back. Thread the remaining end through the other hole. Knot to fit.